NORMAN BRIDWELL

Clifford's
ABC

scarecrow

elephant

dog

elf

ISBN 0-590-44286-4

58 57 56 55 54   14 15 16/0

Printed in the U.S.A.

NORMAN BRIDWELL
Clifford's
ABC

alligator

beaver

cow

SCHOLASTIC INC.
New York   Toronto   London   Auckland   Sydney

Aa

Aa
accordion
acorns
alligator
anchor
ant
anvil
armadillo
axe

axe

accordion

armadillo

anvil

acorns

ant

anchor

alligat

Bb

bird

ball

bat

boots

basket

balloon

boy

boat

butterfly

beaver

bottle

baby

Cc

cactus
cake
candle
cape
cat
checks
clown
collar
cook
cow

collar

cow

cat

cook

candle

cake

cactus

cape

clown

checks

Dd

dragon

dolphin

dog

dummy

derby

drum

dandelion

Ee
eagle
earring
eel
egg
elephant
elf
Eskimo

eagle

egg

earring

elephant

Ee

eel

Eskimo

elf

Ff

flag

frog

fly

fish

fire

fairy

flea

funnel

fox

flower

ghost

gorilla

giraffe

Gg

garden

goat

Gg
garbage can
garden
ghost
giraffe
glove
goat
gorilla

glove

garbage c

Hh

helicopter

harp

house

horse

hollyhock

hummingbird

hat

horn

stack

hippopotamus

Ii

iguana

igloo

iris

ink

iron

ice cream cone

Jj

jet

juggler

jogger

jack-o'-lantern

jester

jacks

Kk L1

Kk
kangaroo
karate
kayak
kitten
knight
knitting
koala

Ll
lamb
lasso
leopard
lily
lion
lobster
log
lumberjack

koala

knight

lobster

lily

lasso

lumberjac

karate

knitting

kitten

log

kangaroo

kayak

leopard

lamb

lion

Mm

moon

mop

map

mask

monkey

mittens

mouse

magician

marionette

magnet

M

Nn
nest
net
noodles
note
nun
nurse
nut
nutcracker

Nn

note

nest

net

nun

nutcracker

nut

nurse

noodles

Oo

owl

orchid

ostrich

octopus

orange

overalls

oar

Pp
paintbrush
palette
palm
panda
parachute
pear
picture
pig
pineapple
pirate
pony
porcupine

parachute

palm

P p

pineapple

picture

pand

paintbr

pirate

pear

palet

pony

pig

porcupine

Qq

quail

quartet

question

queen

quilt

rain

Rr

rainbow

rhinoceros

rocket

robot

rope

racket

Rr
rabbit
raccoon
racket
radishes
rain
rainbow
rake
rhinoceros
robot
rocket
roller skate
rope
rug

rug

raccoon

rabbit

rake

roller skate

radishes

Ss

Saturn

star

scarecrow

sleep

saxophone

soccer ball

sausage

sandwich

seesaw

squirrel

snail

seal

stool

Tt

tepee

tent

tractor

tiger

telescope

televis...

teapot

train

teddy bear

turtle

table

Uu

UFO

umbrella

unicorn

umpire

urn

ukulele

unicycle

Vv

volcano

vampire

valentine

Vv
vacuum cleaner
valentine
vampire
vase
violets
violin
vise
volcano

violets

violin

vise

vacuum cleaner

vase

Ww

whale

waves

walrus

wrenches

wheelbarrow

witch

wolf

worm

waffles

wagon

Xx Yy

Xx
x-ray
xylophone

Yy
yacht
yak
yarn
yawn
yo-yo

xylophone

yacht

x-ray

yak

yawn

yarn

yo-yo

zeppelin

Zz

zebra

zipper

zither

ZOO

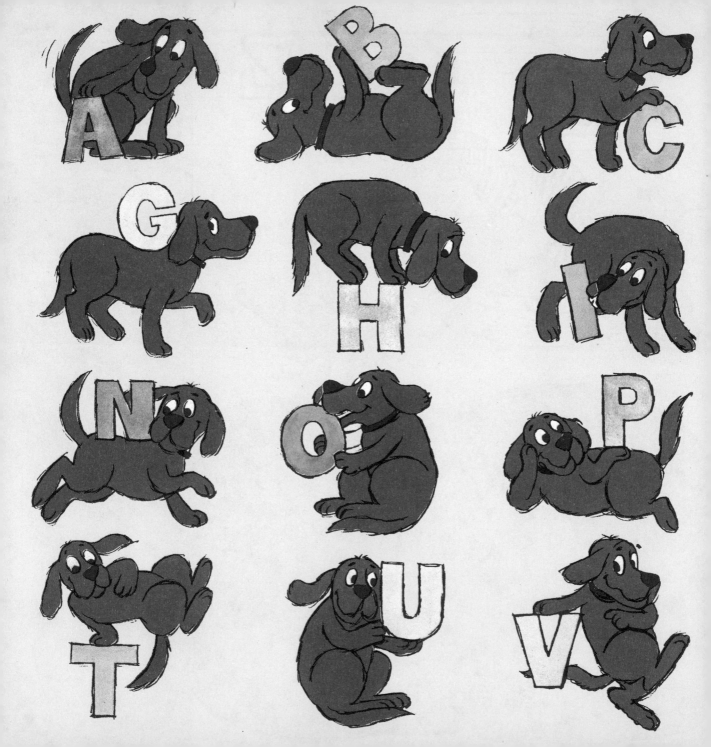